Pinocchio

Pinocchio

By Carlo Collodi
Adapted by Catherine Daly-Weir

Bullseye Step into Classics™

Random House New York

A BULLSEYE BOOK PUBLISHED BY RANDOM HOUSE, INC.
Text copyright © 1996 by Random House, Inc.
Cover illustration copyright © 1996 by Tony Meers

http://www.randomhouse.com/

Library of Congress Cataloging-in-Publication Data:
Daly-Weir, Catherine.
Pinocchio / by Carlo Collodi ; adapted by Catherine Daly-Weir.
   p. cm. — (Bullseye step into classics)
SUMMARY: Pinocchio, a wooden puppet full of tricks and mischief, with a
talent for getting into and out of trouble, wants more than anything else to
become a real boy. ISBN 0-679-88071-2 (pbk.) [1. Fairy tales. 2. Puppets—
Fiction.] I. Collodi, Carlo, 1826–1890. Avventura di Pinocchio. English.
II. Title. III. Series. PZ8.W432Pi 1996 [Fic]—dc20 95-33455

First Random House Bullseye Books edition: 1996

Printed in the United States of America
10 9 8 7 6 5 4 3 2 1

Contents

Contents

Chapter 1

❧❧❧

The Magic Puppet

Once upon a time, a jolly old carpenter found a piece of wood in his workshop. The carpenter's name was Mr. Cherry. He made furniture for the people of his village.

Mr. Cherry needed the piece of wood to make a leg for a table. It was a common piece of wood—the kind used in stoves and fireplaces. But as soon as Mr. Cherry picked the wood up, a tiny voice begged, "Please don't hurt me!"

Mr. Cherry was shocked.

"Who said that?" he demanded, and looked around his workshop. But there was no one else in the room. He looked under the bench—nobody. He looked in the cupboard—no one. He looked in the basket of chips and sawdust. But there was nobody inside!

"I must have imagined that voice," Mr. Cherry said finally, and went back to work. The carpenter picked up a rough piece of sandpaper and began smoothing out the piece of wood.

"Stop it! You're tickling me!" cried the tiny voice.

Mr. Cherry stared at the wood in amazement. He couldn't believe what was happening. The piece of wood was talking to him! Mr. Cherry was so scared that he fell off his stool and landed on the floor.

Just then, someone knocked on Mr. Cherry's door. "Come in!" said the carpenter, as he struggled to his feet. It was his neighbor, Geppetto, a kind woodcarver with a good heart.

"Good morning, Mr. Cherry," Geppetto said. "Perhaps you can help me. I want to make a puppet that will dance and fence and turn somersaults. With this puppet, I could put on a marvelous puppet show. I would be famous and would travel all over the world. I would take very good care of my puppet. I would love him like a son. Do you have a piece of wood for me?"

Mr. Cherry gladly gave Geppetto the talking piece of wood.

"It's yours," he said.

Geppetto knew he could carve the wood into a magnificent puppet. The wood was solid and just the right size. He was anxious to get started, so he thanked Mr. Cherry and headed straight home.

Geppetto was a very poor, lonely man. He lived by himself with only his wooden puppets to keep him company. His house was barely furnished. He owned only a worktable, a chair, a bed, and some tools.

"I think I will name this puppet Pinocchio," Geppetto said as he started shaping the wood. "I once knew a happy family named Pinocchio. It is a lucky name."

As Geppetto worked, strange things began to happen. When he carved the puppet's eyes, they winked at him. When he made the nose, it grew longer and longer. When he carved the mouth, it laughed out loud. When he made the feet, they kicked him in the nose!

Geppetto had never seen a puppet act this way before. Puppets could not move on their own! This was not an ordinary doll, Geppetto decided. Pinocchio must be magical.

When the woodcarver was finished, he took the little puppet by the hand and walked him around the room.

"You're getting good at this," teased Geppetto. "Soon you'll be walking all by yourself. Then you can go to school, like a good little boy."

As soon as Geppetto said those

words, Pinocchio let go of his hand and ran out the door!

Geppetto chased Pinocchio down the street. "Catch him! Catch him!" he cried to his neighbors.

But everyone simply laughed and laughed at the funny wooden puppet running down the street.

When Geppetto finally caught up to Pinocchio, the puppet sat down on the cobblestone street and refused to go home.

Soon a crowd gathered around the magic puppet. A policeman heard the commotion and came by to see what was the matter. Someone told him that Geppetto had been very mean and beat Pinocchio. It wasn't true—but the policeman took Geppetto to jail anyway!

Pinocchio ran home as quickly as he could. He threw open the door and sat down in front of the warm fire. At least *he* was safe. But Pinocchio's relief did not last long.

"Hello," a voice called out.

Pinocchio was scared. "Who is it?" he asked.

"I am a talking cricket," answered the insect. "I have lived in this room for over one hundred years. I have something important to tell you. You should listen to your father. You should go to school and behave. Bad boys who run away and do not obey their parents never come to any good in this world."

But Pinocchio did not want to listen to the cricket's advice. "I will run away again tomorrow," he said. "Then I won't have to go to school."

"If you don't go to school, you will grow up to be a donkey and everyone will laugh at you," replied the cricket.

"Be quiet!" shouted Pinocchio.

"I feel sorry for you," continued the cricket.

"Why?" asked Pinocchio.

"Because you are a puppet with a wooden head."

That was the last straw! Pinocchio lost his temper. He grabbed Geppetto's hammer and threw it at the cricket. The cricket jumped away just in time. He shook his head sadly and disappeared.

Now Pinocchio was all alone, and it was dinnertime. His stomach grumbled noisily. He looked around the room for something to eat, but there was no food to be found—not even a crust of bread. Geppetto's cupboards were bare.

Pinocchio began to cry. "The talking cricket was right," he said. "I should never have run away from my father. If he were here, I wouldn't be dying of hunger right now!" Tired and hungry, Pinocchio fell asleep with his feet on a heater full of burning coal.

Silly Pinocchio forgot that his feet were made of wood! They burned right off during the night.

The next day, Geppetto was released from jail. "Open the door, Pinocchio," he called. Pinocchio woke up and tried to run to the door. But he didn't realize his feet were gone and he tumbled to the floor.

"I can't," cried the little puppet.

Geppetto thought that Pinocchio was playing another trick on him. He climbed through the window, ready to scold the puppet. But then he saw poor Pinocchio lying on the floor, with no feet!

Geppetto picked Pinocchio up and gave the hungry puppet the three pears he had bought for his own breakfast. While Pinocchio was eating, Geppetto carved him a new pair of feet.

Pinocchio was very pleased and promised that he would be a good boy and go to school. Geppetto was overjoyed. He loved having a son to take care of—even though Pinocchio wasn't a real boy.

Geppetto made Pinocchio some new clothes. He made a shirt and pants out of paper, shoes from the bark of a tree, and a hat out of a piece of bread.

Pinocchio reminded his father that there was still one thing missing: a schoolbook.

"I need a book to write my lessons in," said the puppet.

"I'm sorry, Pinocchio," said Geppetto. "But I haven't any money!"

Pinocchio looked so sad. Geppetto wanted to give his son everything his wooden heart desired. So he put on his old coat with all the holes and patches and ran out into the cold. He returned with a book, but no coat.

"Where is your coat?" asked Pinocchio.

"I sold it," said the shivering man. "I didn't need it anymore."

But Pinocchio knew that was not true. Geppetto had sold his only coat to buy Pinocchio a book for school.

"Oh, thank you, Daddy," Pinocchio said, and threw his arms around the old woodcarver. "You are so good to me. I will love you always. I will be the very best son you'll ever have."

Chapter 2

❧

Skipping School

Soon it was time for Pinocchio to go to school. He left home with his new schoolbook under his arm and many dreams in his head.

I'll learn to read and write. I'll be very smart. I'll get a job and earn lots of money and buy fancy clothes for my father, he thought to himself.

Pinocchio's grand daydreams were interrupted by the sound of lively carousel music in the distance.

Somebody is having a marvelous time, thought Pinocchio. *A lot more fun than I would have at school.*

Pinocchio did not know what to do. Should he follow the music and find out where it was coming from? Or should he go to school and keep his promise to Geppetto?

It did not take long for Pinocchio to make his choice. "I'll go to school tomorrow," he said, and hurried toward the music.

After a short walk, Pinocchio found a group of people gathered around a colorful building. He saw a big sign, but he didn't know how to read. A boy told him that the sign said: MAGICAL PUPPET SHOW, ONE DOLLAR.

Pinocchio did not have a dollar. All he had were his schoolbook and the clothes on his back. But he really wanted to see the show. Without a second thought, Pinocchio sold his schoolbook to a peddler for one dollar.

The show had already started when Pinocchio walked in. Two puppets named Harlequin and Punchinello were in the middle of a loud argument. The crowd was roaring with laughter.

The puppets were just like Pinocchio! They could move and talk on their own—without the help of strings or a puppeteer.

Harlequin spotted Pinocchio in the audience right away. All the magical puppets in the village had heard about Geppetto's new puppet. Harlequin stopped the show and shouted, "Pinocchio, is that you?"

"Yes, it's me!" replied Pinocchio.

"Come up here and join your fellow puppets!" Harlequin exclaimed.

Pinocchio jumped onstage. The other puppets came running from the wings, and they all hugged and kissed him. They lifted Pinocchio onto their shoulders and carried him around the stage.

The audience grew restless. "We want to see the play!" they yelled.

Suddenly, the puppet master appeared. He was tall and ugly. His long black beard nearly touched the floor. His mouth was huge, and his eyes glowed red. The puppets called him Fire-eater. At the sight of him, they trembled with fear.

"You have disturbed my theater!" Fire-eater growled at Pinocchio. "I will deal with you later!" Then the puppet master turned and stormed off the stage.

All the puppets scurried back to their places. Pinocchio hopped off the stage, and the show went on.

After the play was over, Pinocchio joined the puppets backstage. Fire-eater returned, angrier than ever.

"I have run out of wood to cook my dinner," he snarled, looking around the room. "Pinocchio, you are made of nice, dry wood. I'll throw you into the fire!"

Fire-eater grabbed Pinocchio's arm and yanked the little puppet off the floor.

"Oh, Daddy, help! Please save me,"

Pinocchio wailed. "I don't want to die!"

When Fire-eater heard Pinocchio's terrified plea, he felt sorry for him. For under his hard ways and rough looks, he was a kindhearted man.

Then Fire-eater sneezed five times in a row. "Achoo! Achoo! Achoo! Achoo! Achoo!"

All the puppets were relieved. They knew that when Fire-eater sneezed, it meant he was sad. Pinocchio would be saved.

Fire-eater set the frightened little puppet down and said, "I feel sorry for your father. He would be very unhappy indeed if I threw you into the fire."

Fire-eater thought for a minute and then rubbed his hands together. "I will have to use one of my own puppets instead. Harlequin, come here!" he called out.

Harlequin gasped and fainted on the floor. Pinocchio knew he had to help his new friend. He immediately threw himself at the puppet master's feet.

"Please pardon poor Harlequin," he begged.

"But I already pardoned *you*," Fire-eater said. "I must have some wood to cook my dinner!"

"Then you must use me," said Pinocchio bravely. "It is not fair for my friend Harlequin to take my place."

That set Fire-eater off again. He sneezed another five times.

"Very well," he said, shaking his head. "I will eat my dinner half-cooked. You are a good, brave boy, Pinocchio."

Fire-eater reached into his pocket and pulled out five shining gold coins. "Give these to your father," he said.

Pinocchio thanked Fire-eater over and over. The puppets were so happy that they danced and sang all night long.

At dawn, Pinocchio left, determined to return home and share the small fortune with his father.

The puppet had not gone very far when he met a fox and a cat standing by the side of the road. The fox had a crutch, and the cat had a white cane and dark glasses. The fox was pretending to be lame, and the cat was pretending to be blind. The pair wanted to trick people into giving them money.

"Good morning, Pinocchio," said the fox.

"How do you know my name?" asked the puppet.

"I know your father, poor old Geppetto," replied the fox.

"Well, he won't be poor anymore," said Pinocchio proudly. He showed the two animals his money. They were so excited by the gold coins that the fox moved the paw that was supposed to be lame, and the cat lowered her glasses to get a better look. But Pinocchio was busy showing off his treasure and he didn't notice.

"How would you like to double your fortune?" asked the fox.

Pinocchio's eyes widened with disbelief. "Double my fortune! What do you mean?" he asked.

"Come with us to a place called the Field of Miracles," the fox said.

Pinocchio paused. "No," he said. "I have to go home and see my father. I have been a very bad boy."

"But you're losing a fortune!" the fox said. "Your five gold pieces could become thousands in one day!"

The fox and the cat explained that the coins could grow into a gold money tree. All Pinocchio had to do was bury the money in the field, pour two large buckets of water over it, and sprinkle it with two pinches of salt. The tree would grow overnight.

Pinocchio couldn't wait to plant his money in the field. He was so glad to have run into the two kind strangers. He forgot all about his father, the schoolbook he had sold, and his plans to return home.

"Okay, let's go!" Pinocchio shouted excitedly, and the three began their journey to the Field of Miracles.

Chapter 3

❧❧

Danger in the Woods

Pinocchio, the fox, and the cat walked and walked all day until they were very tired. As darkness began to fall, they arrived at the Red Crab Inn.

"Let's stop here for a while," said the fox. "We can eat dinner and rest until midnight."

The cat agreed immediately. Pinocchio couldn't wait to get to the Field of Miracles. But he didn't want to be rude, so he went along with the fox's plan.

The fox and the cat ate quite a feast. They had many helpings of chicken and fish, two different kinds of stew, and several desserts. Pinocchio was too excited about the money tree to eat. He asked for some nuts and bread, but he didn't eat one bite.

Afterward, everyone went to bed. The fox told Pinocchio they would wake him up at midnight to continue their journey.

Pinocchio fell asleep right away. He dreamed that he was in the middle of a field full of small trees covered with glittering gold. The branches were swaying in the breeze and calling out to Pinocchio: Take me! Take me! But just as Pinocchio reached out to grab some coins, he was awakened by three loud knocks at the door.

Pinocchio climbed out of bed and opened the door. It was the innkeeper, who had come to tell him it was midnight.

"Are the fox and the cat ready?" asked Pinocchio with a yawn.

"They are gone," said the innkeeper. "The cat received a message that her son had a cold, and she went home to take care of him. They said they will meet you at the Field of Miracles at sunrise."

"Did they pay the bill for last night's dinner?" Pinocchio asked.

"No," replied the innkeeper. "They didn't want to insult a fine gentleman like you."

"I wouldn't have been insulted," Pinocchio grumbled, and he gave the innkeeper one of his gold coins.

Pinocchio was disappointed that he would have to make the journey alone. He hoped that the Field of Miracles was nearby. He could hardly wait to grow a money tree and collect his gold pieces. He knew Geppetto would be so proud of him!

The night was dark and still. Pinocchio could hardly see his hand when he held it in front of his face. He walked slowly and carefully and tried not to make a sound.

Suddenly, a voice broke the silence. "Hello, Pinocchio," it said.

"Who is it?" Pinocchio asked. He was so scared that his little wooden knees knocked together.

"I am the talking cricket, and I have come to give you some more advice. The woods are dangerous at night. Go home to your father and give him the four gold pieces that are left. He misses you very much."

"But tomorrow I will have thousands of gold pieces and my father will be very happy," argued Pinocchio. "I met a cat and a fox who are helping me grow a money tree."

"Beware of people who promise to make you rich," said the cricket. "They are usually cheaters. It is time for you to go home."

"Well, I won't," said Pinocchio stubbornly. "I am going to meet my friends at the Field of Miracles."

"One more thing," continued the

cricket. "Beware of thieves." And with that, he vanished.

"Silly cricket, there's nothing to be afraid of," Pinocchio said, trying to make himself feel better. "If a thief came up to me, I'd tell him to go away and leave me alone."

Just then, Pinocchio heard a rustling noise in the bushes behind him. The puppet was terrified. What if the cricket was right? What if there were robbers in the woods? He didn't know where to hide the gold pieces, so he put them in his mouth, under his tongue.

In the darkness, Pinocchio could barely see the two masked figures jumping out of the bushes toward him. One was tall. The other was short. They grabbed Pinocchio roughly, shouting, "Give us your money!"

Pinocchio couldn't say a word because his mouth was full of gold coins!

"Give us your money or we'll hurt

you and your father," the bigger one said.

"Not my father!" cried Pinocchio. The gold pieces clinked against his wooden teeth as he spoke.

"Spit out your money!" the robbers demanded. Pinocchio closed his lips together tightly. The bigger robber held Pinocchio's arms while the smaller one tried to force his mouth open. The frightened puppet bit the thief's hand. To his surprise, it was furry, just like a cat's paw!

"Owwwwww!" exclaimed the smaller robber.

Startled by the cry, the other robber let go of Pinocchio's arms. Quickly, Pinocchio tucked the gold coins in his pocket and sprinted into the woods. He ran and ran until he couldn't run anymore. Exhausted, he dropped to the forest floor and fell into a deep, dreamless sleep.

Chapter 4

❧❧

The Field of Miracles

In the forest, Pinocchio became very sick. He had a high fever and slept fitfully for many days.

Luckily, a beautiful fairy with blue hair lived in the woods nearby. One day, the Blue Fairy went for a walk and found the little puppet lying on the ground. She clapped her hands twice, and a magnificent carriage appeared.

The Blue Fairy carefully lifted Pinocchio into the carriage and brought him back to her cottage. There, the Blue Fairy and her helper, a snail, nursed Pinocchio back to health.

When Pinocchio finally awoke, he found himself tucked into bed in a pretty little room. The Blue Fairy was sitting by his side. She was very happy that Pinocchio was well.

"How did you end up in the forest?" she asked.

Pinocchio told the Blue Fairy all about the puppet show, the angry puppet master named Fire-eater, the five gold pieces, the fox and the cat, and the two robbers in the woods.

"Where are the gold pieces now?" asked the Blue Fairy.

"I lost them," lied Pinocchio.

All of a sudden, Pinocchio's nose, which was already long, grew two more inches.

The fairy smiled. "Where did you lose them?" she asked.

"In the woods," Pinocchio lied again. His nose grew even longer.

"If you lost the gold nearby, we can find it easily," the fairy said.

"Oh, now I remember!" Pinocchio said quickly. "I swallowed the coins!"

As Pinocchio told the third lie, his nose grew so very long that he could not turn his head without hitting the walls or breaking a window.

The Blue Fairy laughed and laughed.

"Why are you laughing?" asked Pinocchio. He did not think his long nose was very funny.

"I am laughing at all the lies you are telling me," she said. "Every time you lie, your nose grows."

Pinocchio was very embarrassed and tried to hide his head under the covers. But that was impossible. He began to weep, and cried so much that the fairy took pity on him. She clapped her hands, and Pinocchio's nose shrank back to normal size.

Pinocchio was very grateful and thanked the Blue Fairy over and over.

"That's not all," she said. "I have a surprise for you. Your father Geppetto is on his way to this very cottage. He has been searching for you for several days. He will be here shortly."

Pinocchio could not have been happier. "I will go meet him," he said, and jumped out of bed and ran outside.

Pinocchio had just stepped onto the forest path when he heard voices approaching him. It was the fox and the cat! The cat had a bandage on her paw. They were very surprised to see Pinocchio.

"You'll never believe what happened to me after you left," Pinocchio said. "I was attacked by robbers!"

"Oh, how terrible," said the cat as she hid her bandaged paw under her cloak. "I hope you still have your gold."

"Why, yes, I do," said Pinocchio. "Right here in my pocket."

The fox and the cat smiled wickedly at each other.

"Will you still come with us to the Field of Miracles?" asked the fox.

"No, I can't," said Pinocchio. "I am waiting for my father. He should be here soon."

"But it's very close," said the fox. "And think of how proud your father will be when you come home with all those gold pieces!"

The fox convinced Pinocchio to join them, and the three went off again.

Pinocchio quickly discovered that the fox was wrong. The Field of Miracles was *not* close by. The three walked for several hours until they finally reached an ordinary-looking field.

Under the fox's watchful eye, Pinocchio dug a hole, planted his four gold pieces, and covered them with dirt. He watered the spot and sprinkled it with two pinches of salt.

"Now the cat and I must go," said the crafty fox. "Be sure to come back in twenty minutes, and you will see your money tree beginning to bloom!"

"Oh, thank you, thank you!" Pinocchio said. "How can I ever repay you?"

"Your happiness is thanks enough," the cat told the trusting puppet. The fox and the cat wished Pinocchio a good harvest and left. Pinocchio gave the field a final glance and walked back to town by himself.

The minutes ticked by so slowly! At last it was time for Pinocchio to collect his gold. His heart was pounding as he ran back to the Field of Miracles. He thought of all the wonderful things he would buy for himself and his father with the money: a big house, a pony, toys, and all sorts of tasty treats.

When Pinocchio arrived at the field, he could not believe his eyes. The field was as empty as before. There was no money tree in sight—not even a money twig! Pinocchio was extremely confused. What could have gone wrong?

"*Tsk, tsk, tsk,*" a familiar voice said.

Pinocchio spun around and saw the talking cricket!

"You again!" said Pinocchio. "What are you doing here?"

"I am here to offer you more advice. Don't you know that money doesn't grow on trees? You must earn it by working hard with your hands or with your brain," the cricket said.

"I don't understand," said the puzzled puppet.

"While you were gone, the fox and the cat came back and dug up your money," the cricket explained.

Pinocchio's jaw dropped. It couldn't be true! The fox and the cat were his friends. He fell to his knees and began to dig in the dirt. He dug and dug until he had a hole big enough for a haystack. But the cricket was right—his money was gone. Pinocchio felt awful. Not only had he lost the gold, but he had also missed his father's arrival!

From now on, I have to be good, thought

Pinocchio. He took one last look at the gaping hole and headed back to the Blue Fairy's house.

Chapter 5

❧

The Search for Geppetto

Pinocchio walked for hours. By twilight, he was still far from the Blue Fairy's home. He hoped that Geppetto would wait for him.

Pinocchio had not eaten all day, and he was terribly hungry. He noticed some purple grapes growing in a field by the side of the road. They looked delicious. Pinocchio plucked some grapes off the vine and gobbled up the juicy fruit. He had already eaten several handfuls when someone grabbed him by the shoulder.

"Got you!" a farmer exclaimed. "How dare you steal my grapes!"

Even though Pinocchio wept and

begged for forgiveness, the farmer ignored his pleas.

"You have stolen from me, and now you must pay me back," the farmer said. "As payment for the grapes you have eaten, you will be my watchdog. I want to find out who has been stealing my chickens. If you hear anything strange at night, bark and wake me up."

The farmer tied Pinocchio to a doghouse with a long rope and went to bed.

Pinocchio was miserable. Now he would never make it back to the Blue Fairy's house in time to see his father!

"If only I had been a good boy," he moaned, "I would not be in trouble again. Why didn't I stay home with my father?"

There was nothing for the sad little puppet to do but crawl into the doghouse and fall asleep.

There were no robbers that night or the next two nights. But on the fourth night, Pinocchio was awakened by voices.

"Hello," one voice said. "Who are you?"

"Pinocchio," said the puppet. He opened his sleepy eyes. Four weasels were standing in front of him.

"What are you doing here?" one weasel asked.

"I am a watchdog," replied Pinocchio.

"Aha," said the weasel. "Well, I have a deal to make with you. You will let us into the chicken coop once a week to steal chickens. You won't bark or wake up the farmer. In return, we will give you one chicken. Do we understand each other?"

"Oh, I understand," said Pinocchio slyly.

After the four weasels slipped into the chicken coop, Pinocchio locked the door behind them. He barked like a dog: *"Bow-wow-wow-wow-wow!"*

The farmer came running out of his house in his pajamas. He was very pleased that Pinocchio had caught the thieves. He untied Pinocchio and set him free.

"Go home, Pinocchio," he said.

This time, Pinocchio ran straight to the Blue Fairy's house without a single stop. But when he got there, he discovered that the entire house was gone!

Where was the beautiful Blue Fairy? Where was his loving father? Tears streamed down Pinocchio's face. "I should have listened to the cricket," he cried.

Just then, a huge pigeon flew overhead. He heard Pinocchio's sobs and landed next to the puppet.

"What's the matter?" the bird asked.

"I miss my father, Geppetto," Pinocchio said, blowing his nose.

"I saw Geppetto two days ago," said the friendly pigeon. "He was on a beach and he was building a little boat to cross the ocean. He is searching for his son, Pinocchio."

"That's me!" exclaimed Pinocchio. "Where is this beach?"

"Nearly six hundred miles away," replied the pigeon.

"Six hundred miles!" said Pinocchio. "If only I had wings like you!"

The pigeon felt so sorry for Pinocchio that he offered to fly the puppet all the way there.

Pinocchio jumped onto the pigeon's back, and they soared high above the trees. They flew all day long, stopping only once to eat.

Finally, they arrived at the beach. A small crowd had gathered. Everyone was shouting and pointing to a small figure out at sea. Pinocchio squinted into the distance.

"That's my father!" he shouted. Pinocchio jumped up and down, calling Geppetto's name. Geppetto waved back. Try as he might, the woodcarver could not turn his little boat back to shore. The sea was too rough for the old man to handle. Pinocchio was worried. What should he do?

"Poor man!" said a fisherman. "No one can help him now."

"I will save my father!" Pinocchio announced, and dove into the churning water. Since Pinocchio was made of wood, he floated easily and was an excellent swimmer. But even Pinocchio could not overcome the strong ocean currents. He swam for hours. But he could not reach his father.

Night fell, and the weather got worse and worse. It began to rain. Thunder boomed and lightning crashed around him. Pinocchio lost sight of Geppetto's boat.

The sun began to rise. In the distance, Pinocchio saw a long strip of land. It was an island! Pinocchio tried to reach the land, but the tumbling waves tossed him farther and farther away. Just when Pinocchio had almost given up hope, a big wave picked the little puppet up and dumped him on the sandy shore.

The clouds slowly cleared, and the sea became calm and peaceful. Pinocchio stood up and looked in every direction, hoping to spot his father's small boat. But all he could see was the empty ocean. His father was gone. Pinocchio felt very lonely.

Suddenly, Pinocchio saw a big gray dolphin swimming by. He had a friendly face. Pinocchio was happy to see him.

"Hello, Mr. Dolphin. I am Pinocchio. May I have a word with you?" he asked.

"You may even have two, if you'd like," replied the dolphin with a smile.

"Is there a town on this island?" Pinocchio asked.

"Yes, there is," the dolphin said. "It is a bustling place called Busy Bee Town, and it is not far from here. Take the path to your left and you will find it."

"I have another question for you," continued Pinocchio. "In your travels, have you seen a little boat with my father—the best father in the world—in it?"

The dolphin shook his head no. "There is a huge shark in these waters," he said sadly. "Your father may have been swallowed by him."

Pinocchio stared at the dolphin. "How big is he?"

"The shark is as big as a five-story building, and his mouth is so wide he could swallow a train—engine and all," said the dolphin.

"Oh, my goodness!" Pinocchio whispered. This was very bad news. Would he ever see his father again?

"I am sorry, Pinocchio. Good luck to you," said the kind dolphin as he swam away.

Pinocchio watched the dolphin until he was a tiny speck in the distance.

Then he started walking up the path to Busy Bee Town. With every step, he wondered what he would find when he got there.

Chapter 6

❧

Busy Bee Island

As soon as Pinocchio reached town, he understood why it was called Busy Bee. Everyone was hard at work, hurrying back and forth. Pinocchio could tell that this was not a good place for a lazy puppet.

Pinocchio was very, very hungry. There were only two ways for him to get food. He would either have to beg for money or ask for work.

Geppetto had taught him that it was wrong to beg, but Pinocchio did not want to work for his supper. Then he saw a man pulling a cart loaded with coal coming his way. *Surely he would help a starving puppet,* Pinocchio thought.

He hurried over to the stranger and pleaded for some money.

"Certainly," said the tired man. "I will pay you if you help me pull this cart."

"I am not a donkey," said Pinocchio, shocked at the very idea. "I do not pull carts!"

The man shook his head at Pinocchio's stubbornness and walked away with his heavy load.

Pinocchio asked half the town for money, but no one would give him a penny. They all offered him work so he could earn it, but Pinocchio always refused.

Then a kind woman carrying two pails of water told Pinocchio she would give him a fine meal, with dessert, if he would help her carry one of the pails. By this time Pinocchio was starving, so he agreed.

The pail was very heavy. Pinocchio's arms were not strong enough to carry it, so the little puppet balanced it on his head. He tried not to spill a drop.

When they arrived at the woman's house, she fed him a wonderful meal and a delicious dessert.

Pinocchio gobbled down the food as quickly as he could. He wiped his mouth and looked up to thank the good-hearted woman—but she was gone. In her place stood the Blue Fairy!

"It's you!" he shouted. "I am so glad to see you!"

Pinocchio told the Blue Fairy all about his mistakes and how sad he had been when he couldn't find her or Geppetto. He told her how small he had felt swimming in the great blue sea.

"When will I be bigger?" he asked.

"You won't," replied the Blue Fairy gently. "Puppets never grow. They always stay the same size."

"I am tired of being a puppet," complained Pinocchio. "I want to be a real boy!"

"Well," said the Blue Fairy, "then you will have to work very hard."

"What will I have to do?" Pinocchio asked eagerly.

"First you must be a good boy. Good boys obey their elders, study hard, always tell the truth, and get good grades in school."

"School?" said Pinocchio. "I don't like school at all."

"Why not?" the fairy asked.

"Because I don't like to work."

"My child," said the Blue Fairy. "Everybody has to work, rich or poor. Lazy people never amount to anything."

"My father is a hard worker," Pinocchio said. "Do you think I'll ever see him again?"

"I am sure of it," replied the Blue Fairy.

"Oh, good!" said Pinocchio, jumping for joy. "I will make my father proud of me. I will work hard and study in school. I will do whatever it takes to become a real boy."

Pinocchio was true to his word. He started school the very next day. He studied hard, was an excellent student, and was well liked by his schoolmaster.

Pinocchio made friends with all the students, from the obedient children to the troublemakers. Both the Blue Fairy and the schoolmaster tried to warn him about his mischievous friends. But Pinocchio wouldn't listen.

One fine morning, Pinocchio met some of these boys on his way to school.

"Have you heard the news?" they asked. "There's a huge shark near the beach. He's as big as a mountain!"

It must be the shark that the dolphin told me about, thought Pinocchio. "Tell me more!" he begged.

"Come with us," the naughty boys dared. "We're going to the beach to see it right now!"

"I can't," said Pinocchio. "I really want to join you, but I have to go to school first. I'll go to the beach afterward."

The boys laughed at him. "The shark will be gone by then! You have to come now. It's not far away at all!"

Once again, Pinocchio's curiosity got the better of him, and he and the boys ran toward the beach. Pinocchio was the fastest one of all, and had to stop several times so his friends could catch up to him.

When they arrived at the seashore, there was no sign of the enormous shark. The water was still and calm.

"Where is the shark?" Pinocchio asked.

"Maybe he's taking a nap," one of the boys said.

The other boys laughed and laughed. "We played a joke on you, Pinocchio," they said. "We got you to play hooky from school with us."

"But I *like* school!" Pinocchio said.

"We hate school, and if you are our friend, you must hate it, too!" ordered the biggest of the boys. "If you don't, we won't be your friends anymore!"

"I don't want to be friends with boys who play hooky from school and don't study their lessons," Pinocchio said angrily.

The next thing Pinocchio knew, the biggest boy threw one of his schoolbooks at him. Pinocchio ducked, and it sailed harmlessly over his head. Soon all the boys started throwing their books. But Pinocchio was fast on his feet, and they missed him every time. One boy threw the biggest book of all, Pinocchio's dictionary. He missed the puppet, but he hit one of his own friends right on the head!

The boy turned as white as a sheet and fainted onto the sand. The other children were so frightened that they ran away. Pinocchio and the injured boy were the only ones left behind.

"Wake up! Wake up!" Pinocchio begged the unconscious boy. "Oh, why did I listen to my bad friends? What will the Blue Fairy say?"

Pinocchio was sitting by the boy's side when he heard footsteps behind him. It was a policeman and a big police dog.

"Who hurt this boy?" the policeman asked sternly.

"I didn't do it," said the innocent puppet.

"What was he hurt with?" the policeman questioned.

"This book," Pinocchio said, pointing to the heavy dictionary.

"And whom does this book belong to?" the policeman asked.

"Me," Pinocchio answered in a small voice.

The policeman frowned at the puppet. Pinocchio was sure that he was going to be arrested. All the other boys

were gone. And he had admitted the
book belonged to him! In a panic,
Pinocchio spun around and started
running.

Pinocchio headed straight for the
water, with the big police dog chasing
after him.

Chapter 7

A Narrow Escape

Pinocchio ran as fast as his little wooden legs would carry him. He thought he was getting away, but a quick glance over his shoulder proved he was wrong. The big dog was gaining on him! He could feel the dog's hot breath on his neck.

Only a couple more steps... he thought to himself.

The instant Pinocchio was near the water's edge, he made a wild leap into the surf. The big dog tried to stop, but he had been running too fast and tumbled in headfirst with a splash.

The police dog began to paw the water furiously. "Oh, help me, Pinocchio, I don't know how to swim!" he begged as he tried to keep his nose above water.

Pinocchio did not know what to do. Here was his chance to escape—but the poor dog needed his help. Pinocchio knew he had to do something. Geppetto always said that he should do good deeds.

"If I save you, do you promise to stop chasing me?" Pinocchio asked.

"I promise!" vowed the dog.

Pinocchio grabbed the dog's heavy collar and pulled him to safety.

"Thank you for saving my life," said the dog. "If you ever need my help, call and I will be there."

"I will," said Pinocchio, who now realized that the dog was not mean after all. He was just big and fierce-looking.

After Pinocchio was sure the dog was all right, he jumped back into the water and swam away.

When Pinocchio was far down the beach and away from the policeman, he made his way back to shore. All of a sudden, he felt a strange sensation. His whole body was being lifted in the air.

Pinocchio had been caught in a net full of fish! The fish were all shapes and sizes. They flopped and jumped all over Pinocchio. To make matters worse, the net was being pulled in by the scariest fisherman Pinocchio had ever seen. The fisherman had a long green beard that touched his knees, and he looked like a huge sea monster.

At first, the fisherman frightened Pinocchio. But then the puppet realized that he had nothing to worry about. *As soon as the fisherman sees that I'm not a fish, I'll be free in no time,* he thought.

The sea-monster-fisherman dragged the net into a dark and smoky cave. There was a roaring fire inside. A huge frying pan sat next to the fire. The fisherman began pulling out the things he had caught. There were sardines, crabs, anchovies, mullet, whiting—and Pinocchio.

"What kind of fish is this?" the fisherman bellowed, plucking Pinocchio from the net. "I have never seen such a fish in all my life."

"I am not a fish. I am a puppet!" Pinocchio shouted.

"Aha, a puppet fish!" exclaimed the fisherman. "I can't wait to eat you!"

"Eat me?" screeched Pinocchio. "I am not a fish! Don't you see that I talk and reason as you do?"

"Yes, I do," said the fisherman. "And because you are so special, I will allow you to choose the way you will be cooked. Would you like to be fried in oil or stewed in a tomato sauce?"

"If I have the choice," said Pinocchio slowly, "I would prefer to be set free. I want to go home."

"Set you free?" asked the fisherman.

"And miss my chance to eat a puppet fish? No, I will fry you along with all the others. You will enjoy the company."

Pinocchio realized that the fisherman meant business. He began to panic. "Oh, why didn't I go to school today!" he moaned.

Pinocchio tried to escape. He wriggled like an eel in the fisherman's hand, but the fisherman held on tight.

The fisherman tied Pinocchio's arms and legs. He rolled the fish, one by one, in flour and threw them into the frying pan. He picked up Pinocchio last, coated him thoroughly, and dangled him above the sizzling pan.

"Help me! Help me!" cried Pinocchio, desperately hoping that someone would hear him. He was sure the end was near.

From out of nowhere, a dog barked a reply. It was the police dog whose life Pinocchio had saved! The dog ran into the cave, snatched Pinocchio from the fisherman's grasp, and darted out, fast as lightning.

When they reached the road, the dog gently placed Pinocchio on the ground and untied him.

"How did you find me?" asked the puppet.

"I was hungry and smelled the fisherman's dinner. When I got to the cave, I heard your cries," explained the dog.

"How can I ever thank you?" Pinocchio asked.

"There is no need to thank me," said the dog. "You helped me, and now I have helped you."

The two new friends headed down the road. When they reached town, the dog and the puppet shook hands and parted ways.

Pinocchio was not ready to continue his journey. He had to find out what had happened to the boy who had been hurt on the beach.

Pinocchio stopped at a nearby house

and knocked on the door. An elderly gentleman answered.

"Excuse me," Pinocchio said, "but did you hear anything about a schoolboy who was hit on the head today?"

"Yes, I did," said the man. "He is fine now and has gone home."

Pinocchio was happy to hear the good news. "So the wound was not too serious?" he asked.

"Well, it could have been," said the man. "One of his schoolmates threw a heavy book at him. His name is Pinocchio."

"Who is this Pinocchio?" the little puppet asked, pretending he didn't know.

"Oh, they say he is very bad," the man replied, shaking his head.

"That is not true!" Pinocchio exclaimed. "He is good and obeys his father, always goes to school, and is a hard worker."

The moment that Pinocchio lied, his

nose grew several inches longer! The little puppet was alarmed. He had to stop telling so many lies!

"Oh, no, that's not true," Pinocchio added quickly. "Pinocchio is very bad. He doesn't obey his father. He doesn't work hard, and he plays hooky from school."

When Pinocchio told the truth, his nose returned to normal size. He bid the man a hasty farewell and continued on to the Blue Fairy's cottage.

All the way home, Pinocchio was worried. *Will the Blue Fairy forgive me?* he wondered. *This is the second time I have been naughty. It would serve me right if she sent me away.*

It was very late when Pinocchio arrived at the Blue Fairy's house. She was already asleep. Pinocchio had to wait for her helper, the snail, to come open the door. It was a long wait. The snail was on the fourth floor, and she was very slow. Even though she rushed as quickly as she could, it took her nine hours to get downstairs!

After several hours, Pinocchio lost his patience. He kicked the front door, and his foot went straight through the wood! Pinocchio tried to pull his foot out, but he was stuck. He had no choice but to stay that way all night long. Although he was uncomfortable, he was also very tired, and he fell asleep right on the doorstep.

The next morning, Pinocchio woke up and found himself inside the house, lying on a sofa. The Blue Fairy was at his side. She was very angry with him for skipping school. She was also glad he was home safe and sound, and she forgave him.

"Remember, this is the last time, Pinocchio," she warned. "I will not forgive you if you misbehave again."

Once more, Pinocchio promised he would be a good puppet.

Pinocchio kept his word for the rest

of the year. He studied hard and got the best grades in school. The fairy was very proud.

One day, the Blue Fairy told Pinocchio that all his troubles were over. "Tomorrow your wish will be granted," she said. "Tomorrow you will become a real boy."

"Really?" Pinocchio couldn't believe his ears. His dream was finally going to come true!

The good fairy told Pinocchio to invite all his friends over for a party the next day. There would be candy and cake for everyone.

Pinocchio couldn't wait to invite all his friends and tell them the good news. He left the house immediately and promised to be home in an hour.

Pinocchio ran all over town and told everyone of his good fortune—everyone except Lampwick. Lampwick was the laziest and naughtiest of all the boys in school. His real name was

Romeo, but everyone called him Lampwick. He was tall, thin, and bright, just like the wick of an oil lamp.

Lampwick was Pinocchio's best friend. And Pinocchio could not find him anywhere! He searched and searched for Lampwick. He finally found his friend sitting under a neighbor's front porch.

"What are you doing here?" Pinocchio asked.

"I am waiting here until midnight," explained Lampwick. "Then I am going far, far away to live in Playland. It's the most beautiful country in the world. Why don't you come, too?"

"No, thank you," said Pinocchio. "I've come to invite you to a party. Tomorrow I am going to become a real boy, just like you."

"A lot of good it will do you," replied Lampwick. "Boys have to go to school and study and obey their parents and their teachers. In Playland, there are no schools, no teachers, and no books. Nothing to do but have fun all day long."

"No, I really can't go," said Pinocchio. "I promised the Blue Fairy I would be good, and I must go back home. Good-bye, Lampwick."

But Pinocchio didn't leave.

"Are you sure that no one ever has to study in Playland?" he asked.

"Never, never, never," said Lampwick. "In every week there are six Saturdays and one Sunday."

"What a beautiful country," Pinocchio said with a sigh. "Well, good-bye, I must be going!"

But he still didn't move.

"Well, maybe I'll wait to see you off," Pinocchio said. "I'm sure I'm already in trouble for being late, so a little while longer won't really matter."

The two waited and waited until it was very dark. Then they saw lights in the distance and heard bells jingling.

Lampwick and Pinocchio quickly scrambled out from under the porch.

"What is it?" whispered Pinocchio.

"It's the coach to Playland," replied Lampwick. "Are you coming or not?"

"Are you sure there are no books or teachers in Playland?" Pinocchio asked.

"Not a single one," said Lampwick.

The coach stopped in front of them. It was pulled by twelve pairs of donkeys wearing white leather boots. Some of the donkeys were gray. Some had spots. Some had blue and yellow stripes!

A short, fat man with a red face drove the coach. Dozens of children were crammed inside.

Lampwick jumped right in and joined the other happy children, but Pinocchio stayed behind.

"Aren't you coming?" asked the coachman.

"No, I must stay and go to school," said Pinocchio.

"Too bad," said the little man.

"These children will never have to go to school. They will have fun from morning to night."

Pinocchio's promises to the Blue Fairy melted away. He could not fight the temptation any longer. Playland sounded like paradise.

"All right, I'll come," he finally said.

All the children cheered as Pinocchio ran to join them.

Chapter 8

Playland

There was no room in the crowded coach for Pinocchio. He had to ride on one of the donkeys, but he didn't mind. He was busy thinking about all the fun he and Lampwick would have in Playland.

The coach had not traveled far when Pinocchio heard a voice. It was very low, but Pinocchio heard it clearly. The voice said, "You poor fool. You'll be sorry."

Pinocchio was startled and looked around. Who was talking to him? There was no one else around except the donkeys. The coach driver and the children were too far away to talk to him. Pinocchio decided that he must have been hearing things.

A short while later, Pinocchio heard the voice again. "Children who won't study or go to school always end up in a lot of trouble. I know what I am talking about. One day you will cry like me, but it will be too late!"

Now Pinocchio was truly frightened. He jumped off the donkey's back and grabbed the bridle. To his surprise, the donkey was crying!

The coach started moving faster, and Pinocchio hopped back on the donkey's back. He heard the children's merry singing from the coach. Soon he completely forgot about the mysterious voice.

Several hours later, the coach arrived at Playland. Pinocchio could not believe his eyes. There were children everywhere. Some were playing hopscotch. Others were playing tag. Some were playing blindman's buff. Others were playing ball. A theater put on free plays all day long. There were toys and games as far as the eye could see: a merry-go-round, balloons, bicycles, stilts, toy drums, dolls, jacks, and musical instruments of all kinds. The noise was deafening.

The children piled out of the coach in a mad rush. Pinocchio and Lampwick were the first to enter the front gates.

Playland was exactly as Lampwick had promised. Pinocchio never had to do dishes or pick up his clothes. There were no lessons, schoolmasters, or homework to interrupt his fun-filled days. No one told him what to do. Playland *was* paradise!

Then one morning, Pinocchio's happy days ended. When he woke up, he scratched his head and knew something was very wrong.

Pinocchio ran over to the mirror. There were two large, furry donkey ears where his little wooden ears had been!

Pinocchio could not believe it. He screamed for help. He made so much noise that the squirrel who lived upstairs came down to see what was the matter.

"Squirrel, something is wrong with me. Please feel my forehead to see if I have a fever," Pinocchio begged.

The squirrel put her paw on Pinocchio's head and sighed sadly. "I am sorry, my friend," she said, "but I have bad news for you."

"What is it?" Pinocchio asked fearfully.

"You have a dangerous fever," she answered.

"What kind of fever is it?"

"Donkey fever," she said unhappily. "Pretty soon you will no longer be a puppet. You will be a donkey."

"Is there anything I can do to stop it?"

"No," said the squirrel. "No one can

help you now. Everybody knows that lazy children who play all day and don't go to school end up becoming little donkeys."

"This is all Lampwick's fault," said Pinocchio. He ran to his friend's house as fast as he could.

When Lampwick opened the door, Pinocchio discovered that he, too, had long donkey ears! The two boys laughed and laughed at how funny they looked.

All of a sudden, both boys stopped laughing. Their bodies bent over, and they started running around the room on all fours. They grew tails, and their hands and feet became hooves. Pinocchio and Lampwick tried to shout, but all that came out of their mouths were hee-haws!

Pinocchio and Lampwick had become donkeys—just as the talking cricket had predicted long ago.

The coach driver found the two braying donkeys right away. He was a millionaire. He went around the world, tempting children into coming to Playland. The children would play all day. After they turned into donkeys, he sold them for a tidy profit.

The coach driver brushed Pinocchio and Lampwick until their coats gleamed. Then he saddled them up and took them to the market.

Pinocchio and Lampwick were handsome little donkeys. The coach driver had no trouble selling them. Lampwick was bought by a farmer, and Pinocchio was purchased by the manager of a circus.

At the circus, Pinocchio worked hard every day learning new tricks. He was taught how to stand on his hind legs, jump through hoops, and dance to music. His new master hit him every time he made a mistake. At night, Pinocchio was led back to the stables for a meal of water and hay.

If only I had stayed home and gone to school, he thought. *I'd be feasting on one of the Blue Fairy's delicious meals instead of this dry hay. Oh, why wasn't I good? I will never make this mistake again! If I ever get out of here and become a puppet again, I* will *be good.*

After weeks of practice, it was time for Pinocchio's first performance. Colorful posters all over town announced his act. "Come and see the dancing donkey!" they read. The circus tent was packed with boys and girls. They all wanted to see Pinocchio.

The ringmaster made a speech. Then he introduced the star of the show—Pinocchio.

Pinocchio proudly trotted to the center ring. He wore a shiny new bridle and had flowers tucked behind his ears. His mane had beautiful curls, and ribbons were braided in his tail. He was a lovely little animal.

Pinocchio performed wonderfully.

He jumped, ran, danced, and played dead. The audience loved him. They clapped and cheered. One woman clapped the loudest. Pinocchio paused to take a good look at her. It was the Blue Fairy!

Pinocchio was overcome with joy. He tried to cry, "Blue Fairy, it is me, Pinocchio!" But the only thing he could say was, "Hee-haw, hee-haw!"

The crowd laughed loudly, but the ringmaster was not amused. He was furious. He hit Pinocchio on the nose. When Pinocchio turned to look at the fairy for help, she was gone!

Pinocchio remembered the Blue Fairy's last warning. She said she wouldn't forgive him if he disobeyed again—and she meant it! Pinocchio was all alone. He was so upset that he began to cry.

It was time for the show's finale. The ringmaster forced Pinocchio to jump through a hoop. Pinocchio's eyes were filled with tears, and he couldn't see where he was going. He tripped and fell, hurting his leg.

That was Pinocchio's first and last circus performance. The little donkey's dancing days were over.

Chapter 9

❧

Swallowed by a Shark!

The ringmaster did not need Pinocchio any longer. What would he do with a donkey that couldn't dance? A few days later, the ringmaster sold Pinocchio to a farmer. The farmer saddled the little donkey up and led him far away from the colorful circus tent.

Pinocchio's heart grew heavier as he got closer and closer to the farm. He knew that his future would be full of backbreaking work. He was sure he would never see the Blue Fairy or Geppetto again.

The farmer led the donkey across an old rickety bridge. Pinocchio's head hung low, and he did not watch where he was going. He lost his footing on a loose board and fell right into the water!

The farmer grabbed Pinocchio's rope and tugged hard. Pinocchio emerged from the water with the rope still around his neck—but he wasn't a donkey anymore. Pinocchio had turned back into a puppet!

The farmer was stunned. "Where is the little donkey I bought?" he asked.

"I *am* the little donkey," replied Pinocchio with a chuckle.

"Don't play tricks on me!" said the confused farmer, shaking his fist. "You are not a donkey."

"I am very serious," said Pinocchio as he untied the rope. "I used to be a wooden puppet. I was just about to become a real boy when I ran away from home. I went to a terrible place and was lazy and didn't go to school. I was turned into a donkey. Then I was sold to the ringmaster of the circus. He sold me to you. Thank goodness the Blue Fairy changed me back into a puppet! Maybe she has forgiven me again."

"Who is this fairy?" asked the farmer.

"She is my guardian angel," said the puppet. "She loves me and helps me— even when I've been bad."

"This is nonsense!" the farmer shouted. "I want my money back!" He stared at Pinocchio for several seconds. "I know what I will do. I'll sell you for firewood," he finally said, and tried to grab the little puppet.

Pinocchio was too quick for the farmer. He dove into the sea and swam away, waving a merry good-bye.

Pinocchio was so happy to be a puppet again. He splashed around in the water, not paying attention to where he was going.

Suddenly, he looked up and saw a huge sea monster approaching. Its enormous mouth was wide open, and

Pinocchio could see its many rows of sharp white teeth.

Oh, no! thought Pinocchio. *It's the shark! I have to get out of here!*

The puppet tried desperately to swim away, but the huge shark was as quick as an arrow. Pinocchio was no match for the beast's speed or strength. The shark swallowed the puppet up in an instant.

Pinocchio tumbled down the shark's throat, all the way into his stomach. Pinocchio couldn't see a thing. It was as dark as diving headfirst into a bottle of ink. He felt a cold breeze blowing from the shark's lungs.

"Oh, help me!" Pinocchio shouted in a panic.

"You can yell all you want, but there is no one to save you," said a funny little voice.

"Who are you?" Pinocchio asked, trembling.

"I am a tuna fish," the voice replied.

"The shark swallowed us at the same time."

"My name is Pinocchio. How are we going to get out of here?"

"Oh, we can't," said the fish sadly. "This is the end of the line. We are stuck in here forever."

"That can't be true," said Pinocchio. "There must be a way to escape."

"You can try," said the tuna. "But I don't think there is a way out."

As they were talking, Pinocchio saw a gleam of light twinkling in the distance.

"What can that be?" he wondered aloud. "Maybe it is a fish who can tell me how to get out of here."

The tuna fish wished Pinocchio good luck, and the little puppet forged ahead in the darkness. He tried to be brave as he searched for the light ahead. He walked nearly a mile before he reached the dim, flickering light.

Way down at the bottom of the shark's stomach, Pinocchio saw a table with a lighted candle and a little white-haired old man.

Could this be his long-lost father, Geppetto? The man looked ten years older than the happy woodcarver he remembered. He took a step closer and peered at the man.

"Daddy, it's you!" Pinocchio cried. "I'll never, ever, ever leave you again!" Pinocchio ran to the old man and threw his arms around his neck.

"Pinocchio," said Geppetto in a shaky voice. "Is it really you?" The old man rubbed his eyes in disbelief.

"It is really, truly me," said Pinocchio. He told Geppetto about all the terrible things that had happened to him—all because he was bad.

When Pinocchio finished his story, Geppetto told him about his search on land and sea for his son. A giant wave had upset his boat. The shark had swallowed him on the same stormy night he saw Pinocchio on the beach.

"What did you eat all this time?" asked Pinocchio in amazement. It had been nearly two whole years since that night!

"Lucky for me," said Geppetto, "the shark swallowed an abandoned ship full of canned food, fresh water, raisins, cheese, coffee, sugar, candles, and matches. I have been able to live on these things for two years, but now my supplies have run out. This is the very last candle."

"Then there is no time to lose," said Pinocchio. "We must escape tonight after the shark falls asleep."

"Escape—but how?" asked Geppetto. "No one has ever escaped since I've been here."

"We must escape through the shark's mouth and swim away," Pinocchio replied.

"There's only one problem," said Geppetto. "I can't swim."

"But I can," said Pinocchio. "I am an

excellent swimmer. I will carry you to shore on my back."

"It won't work, my son," said Geppetto sadly. "You are only three feet tall. You are not strong enough to carry me."

"We will see," said Pinocchio. He was determined to leave that very night. He and Geppetto had been separated for too long already. Pinocchio did not want to spend a single night inside the shark.

When he heard the shark begin to snore, Pinocchio knew it was time to make their escape. Pinocchio grabbed the candle from the table, and he and Geppetto tiptoed through the shark's gigantic body until they reached his mouth.

To their surprise, they discovered that the shark slept with his mouth wide open.

This is going to be easy! thought Pinocchio. He led Geppetto past the shark's huge tongue. The night was clear, and they could see the moon and stars reflected in the calm ocean.

Just as they were about to jump into the sea, the shark sneezed! The force of the sneeze knocked Pinocchio and Geppetto back down into the shark's stomach. Once again, father and son carefully made their way back to the shark's mouth.

Geppetto was scared, but Pinocchio took his hand and led him up the throat and along the tongue. They balanced themselves on the shark's sharp teeth.

Geppetto climbed on Pinocchio's back, and the two jumped into the sea. The shark was sleeping soundly and never woke up.

Pinocchio swam as quickly as he could. After a few minutes, Geppetto began to shiver. He was tired, cold, and scared.

"Don't worry, Daddy," said Pinocchio. "We are together now."

"But when will we reach land?" asked Geppetto. "I can't see anything but water and sky."

"We're almost there. I can see land," said Pinocchio, trying to calm his father. But Pinocchio was also getting worried. The shore was still a great distance away, and he was getting tired. He swam and swam, but they never seemed to get any closer.

Finally, Pinocchio was too exhausted to go on. "Daddy, help me. I am so tired," he said.

Pinocchio and Geppetto clung to each other desperately. *What will happen to us now?* thought Pinocchio.

At that moment, a funny little voice spoke up. "Who needs help?" it asked.

"We do!" Pinocchio shouted.

"Pinocchio, is that you?" the voice asked.

"Yes. And who are you?"

"I am the tuna fish, your grateful

friend from inside the shark's stomach."

"How did you escape?" Pinocchio asked.

"You showed me the way, and I followed you out. Here, sit on my back and I will carry you to land," the tuna said.

The tuna fish swam much faster than Pinocchio. It took only four minutes to reach the shore that had seemed so far away before!

Pinocchio jumped off the tuna's back and helped his father down.

"You have saved my father's life," Pinocchio told the fish. "I cannot thank you enough." He gave the fish a big hug and kiss.

The tuna was so moved by Pinocchio's thanks that he couldn't say a word. He quickly dove underwater and swam away.

The sun rose in the morning sky. Pinocchio put his arm around his father, and the two slowly began to walk. They hoped to find a house where they could ask for some food and a place to rest.

They had not gone far at all when they passed two beggars on the road. Pinocchio could not believe his eyes.

It was the fox and the cat!

Chapter 10

❧❧

Real at Last!

"Pinocchio, my good friend!" said the fox. "It is wonderful to see you!"

"Wonderful!" agreed the cat.

The life of crime had not treated the fox and the cat well. They used to pretend to be blind and lame. Now it was true.

"Pinocchio, won't you please give us some money?" begged the fox.

"Have pity on us," said the cat.

"I don't have a penny to my name," said Pinocchio, "because I listened to you thieving rascals! You tricked me and stole from me. I won't be fooled by you anymore."

Pinocchio took his father by the arm

and left the two robbers by the side of the road.

Soon they came to a cheerful little house in the middle of a lovely meadow. It was a simple home with a straw roof, but it looked warm and inviting.

Pinocchio knocked on the door. "Who is it?" asked a familiar voice.

"A poor father and his son," said Pinocchio.

"Come in," the voice said.

Pinocchio and Geppetto walked in, but they didn't see anyone in the cottage.

"Where are you?" asked Pinocchio.

"Up here."

Pinocchio and Geppetto looked up. On the beam near the roof sat the talking cricket!

"Oh, my dear cricket!" said Pinocchio.

"So now I am 'dear cricket,'" the insect said. "Remember when you chased me away from your home by throwing Geppetto's hammer at me? You were very mean to me."

"Forgive me, cricket," said Pinocchio. "I have changed my ways. You can chase me away if you like, but please take pity on my father. He is old and weak."

"I shall take pity on you both," said the cricket. "But I hope you will always remember to treat everyone with kindness. Just as you would like to be treated yourself."

"I will," said Pinocchio, and he meant it.

Pinocchio put his tired father to bed. He needed to find food for Geppetto, but he didn't have any money. Pinocchio remembered how he had once begged for money because he was too lazy to work for it. This time, Pinocchio decided to earn it.

Pinocchio left the cottage and wandered down the road. Not far away, he came upon a large farm. Pinocchio knocked on the barn door and asked the farmer for work. He begged the farmer to help him feed his poor sick father.

The man told Pinocchio that if he drew one hundred buckets of water, he would give him food for his father. Pinocchio worked harder that day than he ever had in his life.

Pinocchio helped the farmer every day for five months. He learned how to weave baskets, and he sold them at the market for extra money. He and his father lived a quiet, peaceful life. Pinocchio did everything for Geppetto, who was still ill. He even built a little cart to take Geppetto out for rides in the country air when the weather was pleasant.

In the evenings, the little puppet studied and practiced his reading and writing.

Pinocchio worked so hard that he

saved enough money to buy a new suit for himself. The puppet was on his way to the market when he spotted a snail coming from the other direction.

"Don't you remember me, Pinocchio?" the snail asked.

"I'm not quite sure," said Pinocchio.

"I am the Blue Fairy's helper," she said. "Remember when I came downstairs to let you in her house and your foot was stuck in the door?"

"Oh, yes!" Pinocchio shouted. "I remember everything! How *is* the Blue Fairy? Does she remember me? Is she still angry with me? Is she far from here? Can I see her?" He was so excited, he almost forgot to breathe!

"My dear Pinocchio," the snail said slowly. "The Blue Fairy is very sick. She is in the hospital, and she has no money at all."

"Oh, not my poor fairy!" Pinocchio moaned. "Take this money to her," he said, handing over each and every penny he had. "I will bring you more tomorrow."

Pinocchio hurried back home. When Geppetto asked him where his new suit was, Pinocchio replied, "I decided I didn't need new clothes after all."

The puppet worked an extra two hours at the farmer's that night and made twice as many baskets when he got home.

Exhausted, he collapsed into bed. That night he dreamed about the Blue Fairy. She was as beautiful as ever. She smiled at Pinocchio and said, "Brave Pinocchio! In return for your good heart, I forgive you all your past misdeeds. Children who love their parents and help them when they are sick and poor are worthy of praise and love. You have learned how to do good deeds. Be good in the future and you will be happy."

Pinocchio woke up, amazed at his dream. But something had changed!

His arms and legs were no longer stiff and jointed. In fact, he felt different all over!

Pinocchio ran over to the mirror. Instead of a little wooden face with painted-on hair and eyes, a handsome face with light brown hair and bright blue eyes stared back at him. Pinocchio was no longer a puppet—he was a real boy at last!

Pinocchio stepped away from the mirror and looked around him. The humble cottage was now a lovely house. The walls were beautifully painted and papered. Brand-new furniture filled the room. A new set of clothing was on the dresser.

Pinocchio put on the suit, cap, and shining new boots. He put his hand in his pocket and found a change purse. Written on it were the words: THE BLUE FAIRY RETURNS PINOCCHIO'S MONEY AND THANKS HIM FOR HIS GOOD HEART. Inside the purse were twenty gold pieces—

much more than he had given the snail.

Pinocchio ran to wake Geppetto. But instead of finding the tired old man who had gone to bed the night before, Pinocchio discovered that Geppetto was as healthy and active as he had ever been. He had taken up woodcarving again and was working on a beautiful mantelpiece. It had leaves and flowers carved into it.

Pinocchio hugged and kissed his father. "Daddy, how did this happen?" he asked.

"Well, Pinocchio," said his father, "when naughty children change their ways, good things happen to the whole family."

"And where is the wooden puppet I used to be?" Pinocchio wondered.

Geppetto pointed to a large puppet leaning against a chair in the corner. The puppet's head was leaning to one side. The arms were dangling, and the legs were bent in different directions. It was a miracle the puppet didn't fall over onto the floor.

Pinocchio laughed out loud with happiness.

"How silly I was when I was a puppet," he said. "And how happy I am to have become a real boy!"

Geppetto hugged his son, and the two lived happily ever after.

Carlo Collodi was born in Florence, Italy, in 1826. His real name was Carlo Lorenzini, but he wrote under the pen name Collodi. Collodi was the name of the little village where his mother was born.

Collodi's career began in the newspaper business. He wrote many articles for Italian newspapers and magazines. Then, one day, a friend told Collodi that he should write stories for children. Collodi tried it and became very successful. Children loved his stories—especially his most famous work, *Pinocchio*.

Carlo Collodi died in 1890 at the age of sixty-four.

Catherine Daly-Weir was born in Queens, New York. Ms. Daly-Weir is the author of several children's books. She lives in a converted brick mill in central Maine with her husband, Richard, and their two cats, Felix and Oscar.

Collect the entire STEP INTO CLASSICS™ series!

You can find more Step into Classics™ wherever books are sold...

OR

*You can send in this coupon (with check or money order)
and have the books mailed directly to you!*

❑	THE ADVENTURES OF TOM SAWYER (0-679-88070-4)	$3.99
❑	ANNE OF GREEN GABLES (0-679-85467-3)	$3.99
❑	BLACK BEAUTY (0-679-80370-X)	$3.99
❑	THE HUNCHBACK OF NOTRE DAME (0-679-87429-1)	$3.99
❑	KIDNAPPED (0-679-85091-0)	$3.99
❑	KNIGHTS OF THE ROUND TABLE (0-394-87579-6)	$3.99
❑	THE LAST OF THE MOHICANS (0-679-84706-5)	$3.99
❑	LES MISÉRABLES (0-679-86668-X)	$3.99
❑	A LITTLE PRINCESS (0-679-85090-2)	$3.99
❑	LITTLE WOMEN (0-679-86175-0)	$3.99
❑	MYSTERIES OF SHERLOCK HOLMES (0-394-85086-6)	$3.99
❑	OLIVER TWIST (0-679-80391-2)	$3.99
❑	PETER PAN (0-679-81044-7)	$3.99
❑	PINOCCHIO (0-679-88071-2)	$3.99
❑	ROBIN HOOD (0-679-81045-5)	$3.99
❑	THE SECRET GARDEN (0-679-84751-0)	$3.99
❑	THE THREE MUSKETEERS (0-679-86017-7)	$3.99
❑	THE TIME MACHINE (0-679-80371-8)	$3.99
❑	TREASURE ISLAND (0-679-80402-1)	$3.99
❑	20,000 LEAGUES UNDER THE SEA (0-394-85333-4)	$3.99

Subtotal	$	_____
Shipping and handling	$	3.00
Sales tax (where applicable)	$	_____
Total amount enclosed	$	_____

Name _____

Address _____

City _____**State** _____**Zip** _____

Make your check or money order (no cash or C.O.D.s) payable to Random
House and mail to: Bullseye Mail Sales, 400 Hahn Road, Westminster, MD 21157.

Prices and numbers subject to change without notice. Valid in U.S. only.
All orders subject to availability. Please allow 4 to 6 weeks for delivery.

**Need your books even faster? Call toll-free 1–800–793–2665
to order by phone and use your major credit card.
Please mention interest code 049–20 to expedite your order.**